Beginner's Book of Wildflowers

With 32 Stickers

Dot Barlowe

Dover Publications, Inc.
Mineola, New York

Copyright

Copyright © 2000 by Dover Publications, Inc.
All rights reserved under Pan American and International Copyright Conventions.

Published in Canada by General Publishing Company, Ltd., 30 Lesmill Road, Don Mills, Toronto, Ontario.

Bibliographical Note

Beginners Book of Wildflowers: With 32 Stickers is a new work, first published by Dover Publications, Inc., in 2000.

DOVER *Pictorial Archive* SERIES

This book belongs to the Dover Pictorial Archive Series. You may use the designs and illustrations for graphics and crafts applications, free and without special permission, provided that you include no more than four in the same publication or project. (For permission for additional use, please write to Permissions Department, Dover Publications, Inc., 31 East 2nd Street, Mineola, N.Y. 11501.)

However, republication or reproduction of any illustration by any other graphic service, whether it be in a book or in any other design resource, is strictly prohibited.

International Standard Book Number: 0-486-41060-9

Manufactured in the United States of America
Dover Publications, Inc., 31 East 2nd Street, Mineola, N.Y. 11501

INTRODUCTION

What a dull world this would be for us all if the magnificent fields of wildflowers, ever changing with the seasons, were not part of our landscape. Hidden in woodlands, growing in profusion along streams and the edges of ponds, or floating gracefully in the ponds themselves, the colorful, often fragrant wildflowers add charm and beauty wherever they grow. Surprisingly, even a crack in city concrete can produce a brilliant yellow dandelion; or from a dry-as-desert beach, a gorgeous, sweet-smelling Rugosa rose may bloom.

This book, with its 32 flower stickers, can be the beginning of a lifetime of observing wildflowers. When you identify the flower you have found, there is room alongside the text to place the sticker that matches it by number. Indexes of both common and scientific names can be found at the end of this book. A short walk from where you are will turn up a beautiful wildflower or two that you have always thought were merely weeds. Good hunting!

Jack-in-the-Pulpit
Arisaema triphyllum

Sticker #1

Height: 2 feet.

Size of Flower: Hooded leaf curves over a spike of tiny flowers (jack), 3 to 4 inches.

Habitat: Rich woodland, damp soil on rocky slopes.

Blooms: April to June.

Range: Throughout eastern United States.

Remarks: Also called Indian Turnip. Native Americans found medicinal use for: headache, ringworm, rheumatism and other ills. Plant becoming rare.

My Observations

Date seen: _____

Locality: _____

Notes:

Fragrant Water Lily
Nymphaea odorata

Sticker #2

Height: Leaves and flowers float on water surface.

Size of Flower: 3 to 6 inches.

Habitat: Pools in bogs, ponds, quiet water.

Blooms: June through mid-autumn.

Range: Throughout eastern United States.

Remarks: Sweetly fragrant, can be pink or white. Leaves semi-round. Flowers and buds when young can be boiled and eaten with melted butter.

My Observations

Date seen: _____

Locality: _____

Notes:

Oxeye Daisy
Chrysanthemum leucanthemum

Sticker #3

Height: 1 to 3 feet.

Size of Flower: 2 inches across.

Habitat: Roadsides, pastures, fields and waste places.

Blooms: June through August.

Range: Throughout the United States, less common in South.

Remarks: Brought from Europe and Asia. Escaped from cultivation. Also called Bruisewort. Its crushed leaves are reputed to cure bruises; its juice supposedly cures gout.

My Observations

Date seen: _____

Locality: _____

Notes:

Indian Pipe
Monotropa uniflora

Sticker #4

Height: 3 to 10 inches.

Size of Flower: ½ to 1 inch.

Habitat: Rich, moist woodland in leaf mold.

Blooms: June through August.

Range: Throughout eastern United States.

Remarks: This parasitic plant lacks chlorophyll. It can be pink or white. Obtains sustenance by feeding on fungi on roots of green plants. Also called Corpse Plant. Was used for eye ailment in colonial times.

My Observations

Date seen: _____

Locality: _____

Notes:

Queen Anne's Lace
Daucus carota

Sticker #5

Height: 1 to 5 feet.

Size of Flower: 1 umbel (cluster of flowers) 3 to 4 inches across.

Habitat: Waste areas, dry fields, roadsides.

Blooms: June through October.

Range: Throughout United States and southern Canada.

Remarks: Common, though handsome weed of Eurasian origin. The small flower in the center of the cluster is purple. Also called Wild Carrot. Native Americans used plant to cure liver and other ailments. The resemblance to Queen Anne's lace headdress brought about its common name.

My Observations

Date seen: _____

Locality: _____

Notes:

Japanese Honeysuckle
Lonicera japonica

Sticker #6

Height: Vine to 30 feet or more.

Size of Flower: 1¼ to 1½ inches.

Habitat: Roadsides, woodland borders, heavy thickets.

Blooms: April to early summer.

Range: New York, Massachusetts, Indiana, Ohio and south to Florida, westward to Kansas and Texas.

Remarks: Imported from Asia. Flowers very sweet smelling. This vine can be a nuisance weed and is extremely fast growing. Its foliage is evergreen.

My Observations

Date seen: _____

Locality: _____

Notes:

Common Dandelion
Taraxacum officinale

Sticker #7

Height: 2 to 20 inches.

Size of Flower: Up to 1½ inches.

Habitat: Lawns, waste places, fields, roadsides and open woodlands.

Blooms: Spring to September.

Range: Throughout country, though rare in southeastern United States.

Remarks: Considered a weed, but leaves gathered as salad greens and flowers brewed for dandelion wine. Medicinally used for jaundice, indigestion and other ills.

My Observations

Date seen: _____

Locality: _____

Notes:

Prickly Pear Cactus
Opuntia humifusa

Sticker #8

Height: Plant reclines, stem composed of 3 inch flattened, oval joints, 1 inch high.

Size of Flower: 2 to 3 inches.

Habitat: Sandy areas, dunes, rocky places.

Blooms: June through August.

Range: Minnesota, southern Ontario, Massachusetts, south to Florida and west to Oklahoma.

Remarks: Only cactus in eastern United States and Canada. Two other varieties of same species in west. Care in handling required as barbed hairs (glochids) can cause worse problems than thorns.

My Observations

Date seen: _____

Locality: _____

Notes:

Common Buttercup
Ranunculus acris

Sticker #9

Height: 2 to 3 feet.

Size of Flower: 1 inch.

Habitat: Fields, lawns, meadows and roadsides.

Blooms: Spring to September.

Range: Labrador to Alaska; south to North Carolina, West Virginia, Missouri and north to Oregon.

Remarks: A naturalized European import. Also called Tall Buttercup, it is the tallest of buttercups. Its juice has a bitter taste, thus discouraging browsing animals and preserving the species.

My Observations

Date seen: _____

Locality: _____

Notes:

Black-eyed Susan
Rudbeckia hirta

Sticker #10

Height: 1 to 3 feet.

Size of Flower: 2 to 3 inches.

Habitat: Fields, open woodlands, waste areas, roadsides, prairies.

Blooms: June through October.

Range: Manitoba, Nova Scotia and southwest to Colorado and Texas.

Remarks: This is a native of our western prairies that spread to our eastern range. Possible antibiotic properties from plant juices.

My Observations

Date seen: _____

Locality: _____

Notes:

Common Sunflower
Helianthus annuus

Sticker #11

Height: To 10 feet.

Size of Flower: 3 to 6 inches.

Habitat: Roadsides, prairies, bottomlands and waste areas.

Blooms: July through October.

Range: Throughout the United States.

Remarks: This plant established in the east from western United States. Flowerhead follows the sun. Native Americans used roasted seeds for preparation of flour for bread, and oil for cooking.

My Observations

Date seen: _____

Locality: _____

Notes:

Butter-and-eggs
Linaria vulgaris

Sticker #12

Height: 1 to 3 feet.

Size of Flower: 1 inch.

Habitat: Roadsides, waste areas, fields.

Blooms: May through October.

Range: Throughout the United States.

Remarks: European import. Orange lip is attractive to bees and some moths for nectar. Can become a nuisance weed. Also called Toadflax.

My Observations

Date seen: _____

Locality: _____

Notes:

Sweet Goldenrod
Solidago odora

Sticker #13

Height: 1½ to 3 feet.

Size of Flower: ⅛ of an inch.

Habitat: Open, dry woodlands and fields.

Blooms: July through September.

Range: New England to Florida, and westward to Oklahoma and Texas, north to Missouri and Ohio.

Remarks: Leaves, when crushed, smell like licorice and make an interesting tea when brewed.

My Observations

Date seen: _____

Locality: _____

Notes:

Tiger Lily
Lilium tigrinum

Sticker #14

Height: 2 to 5 or 6 feet.

Size of Flower: 5 inches, in clusters of 12–20 flowers.

Habitat: Roadsides, woodlands and meadows.

Blooms: July to early autumn.

Range: Throughout eastern United States, garden escapee.

Remarks: Eastern Asian native. Bulbs valued by Chinese as medicine, used by Japanese as vegetable. Smaller bulbs at base of leaves can propagate new plants.

My Observations

Date seen: _____

Locality: _____

Notes:

Northern Pitcher Plant
Sarracenia purpurea

Sticker #15

Height: Flower stem, 1 to 2 feet, pitchers 4 to 10 inches.

Size of Flower: 1½ to 2 inches.

Habitat: Sphagnum and peat bogs.

Blooms: May through August.

Range: Labrador, south coastally to New Jersey, Delaware, Maryland and Florida. West to the Great Lakes and Canadian Rockies, southeast to Iowa and Kentucky.

Remarks: Carnivorous plant: insects trapped in pitchers containing water and plant secretions provide, through enzyme action, nitrogen compounds necessary for plant survival.

My Observations

Date seen: _____

Locality: _____

Notes:

Wild Columbine
Aquilegia canadensis

Sticker #16

Height: 1 to 2 feet.

Size of Flower: 1 to 2 inches.

Habitat: Open rocky slopes, sandy cliffs and rocky woodlands.

Blooms: April to July.

Range: Ontario, Quebec, New England south to Florida, west to the Mississippi.

Remarks: Native Americans ate the boiled roots in times of famine. Powdered seeds believed a love potion by some tribes when rubbed on hands. Also called Rock Bells, Jack-in-Trouser and Rock Lilly.

My Observations

Date seen: _____

Locality: _____

Notes:

AFTER ALL THE STICKERS HAVE BEEN PLACED IN THE CORRECT SPACES, PLEASE GENTLY REMOVE AND DISCARD THESE TWO PAGES.

AFTER ALL THE STICKERS HAVE BEEN PLACED IN THE CORRECT SPACES, PLEASE GENTLY REMOVE AND DISCARD THESE TWO PAGES.

41060-9

Cardinal Flower
Lobelia cardinalis

Sticker #17

Height: 2 to 5 feet.

Size of Flower: 1½ inches.

Habitat: Wet areas, along streams, rich, damp woodlands, meadows and swamps.

Blooms: July through autumn.

Range: Quebec, New Brunswick, Minnesota, Michigan, south to Florida and west to eastern Texas.

Remarks: These flowers are pollinated by small bees and hummingbirds. Their brilliant red recalls the red robes of Catholic Cardinals, therefore the common name. Juice of this plant is poisonous.

My Observations

Date seen: _____

Locality: _____

Notes:

Indian Paintbrush
Castilleja coccinea

Sticker #18

Height: 1 to 2 feet.

Size of Flower: 1 inch.

Habitat: Roadsides, meadows, fields and open woodlands.

Blooms: Late April to August.

Range: From lower Manitoba through New Hampshire, south to Florida and westward to Oklahoma.

Remarks: Can be parasitic on other plants. Used as a tea by Native Americans to cure the common cold. Also called Indian Cup and Indian Pink.

My Observations

Date seen: _____

Locality: _____

Notes:

Bull Thistle
Cirsium vulgare

Sticker #19

Height: To 6 feet.

Size of Flower: 1½ to 2 inches.

Habitat: Roadsides, clearings, waste spaces, fields.

Blooms: June through September.

Range: Throughout.

Remarks: A European import, also called Spear Thistle, is extremely spiny. Use gloves to handle. The root when roasted or boiled makes nutritious fare.

My Observations

Date seen: _____

Locality: _____

Notes:

Pink Lady's Slipper
Cypripedium acaule

Sticker #20

Height: 6 to 15 inches.

Size of Flower: 2 to 2½ inches.

Habitat: Dry, acid woodlands, occasionally wet bogs and swamps.

Blooms: April to July.

Range: Ontario to Newfoundland, northern U.S. to Minnesota, south to South Carolina and Georgia in mountains, and westward to Tennessee.

Remarks: <u>ENDANGERED, Do not pick!</u> Does not do well in gardens. Largest American orchid, also called Moccasin Flower and Stemless Lady's Slipper. A white variety is seen rarely.

My Observations

Date seen: _____

Locality: _____

Notes:

Shooting Star
Dodecatheon meadia

Sticker #21

Height: 8 to 24 inches.

Size of Flower: 1 inch.

Habitat: Open woods, prairies, meadows.

Blooms: April to June.

Range: Wisconsin, west to Pennsylvania, south to Georgia, westward to east Texas.

Remarks: Leaves in a rosette at base of long stalk, flowers in cluster at top. Also called: Indian Chief, Birdbills, Johnny Jump and Roosterheads; pioneers called it Prairie Pointers. Flowers sometimes white.

My Observations

Date seen: _____

Locality: _____

Notes:

Red Clover
Trifolium pratense

Sticker #22

Height: 6 to 15 inches.

Size of Flower: ⅜ inch.

Habitat: Lawns, roadsides, fields and clearings.

Blooms: Spring to September.

Range: Throughout United States and southern Canada.

Remarks: Pasture or hay crop. Was imported from Europe. Clover improves fertility of soil as it stores nitrogen in root nodules. Native Americans and early settlers used it medicinally.

My Observations

Date seen: _____

Locality: _____

Notes:

Purple Loosestrife
Lythrum salicaria

Height: 2 to 4 feet.

Size of Flower: ½ to ¾ inch.

Habitat: Marshes, ditches, wet meadows, flood plains.

Blooms: June through September.

Range: Newfoundland, Quebec, Nova Scotia, New England southward to North Carolina, west to West Virginia, Ohio, Indiana, Missouri and Minnesota.

Remarks: A European import, when massed makes spectacular show for miles in wetlands. Young leaves used as a vegetable in emergency by Native Americans.

My Observations

Date seen: _____

Locality: _____

Notes:

Common Milkweed
Asclepias syriaca

Height: 2 to 5 feet.

Size of Flower: ½ inch.

Habitat: Waste places.

Blooms: June through August.

Range: Saskatchewan to New Brunswick, southward to Georgia, then west to Tennessee, Kansas and Iowa.

Remarks: Larvae of Monarch butterfly eats only milkweed leaves. Chemicals from leaves are transferred to larvae and hence to the butterflies, making these insects poisonous to predatory birds.

My Observations

Date seen: _____

Locality: _____

Notes:

Rugosa Rose
Rosa rugosa

Sticker #25

Height: 3 to 6 feet.

Size of Flower: 2 to 3½ inches.

Habitat: Sand dunes, seashores and roadsides.

Blooms: June to early autumn.

Range: Minnesota to Quebec and New Brunswick, southward to New York and New Jersey coasts.

Remarks: Flowers very fragrant; can be white as well as deep pink. Also called Wrinkled Rose. This rose blooms throughout summer season. Often used to stabilize beaches and dunes.

My Observations

Date seen: _____

Locality: _____

Notes:

Bird's-foot Violet
Viola pedata

Sticker #26

Height: 4 to 10 inches.

Size of Flower: ¾ to 1 inch.

Habitat: Sunny, dry sandy fields, rocky slopes and open woodlands.

Blooms: Early spring to June.

Range: Ontario, Minnesota, Michigan, Massachusetts, New York and south.

Remarks: This violet may be entirely light violet-blue. Its bicolored variety (shown here) is considered the most beautiful of all violets. Deeply cut leaves look like a bird's foot, suggesting its common name.

My Observations

Date seen: _____

Locality: _____

Notes:

Chicory
Cichorium intybus

Sticker #27

Height: 3 to 5 feet.

Size of Flower: 1 to 1½ inches.

Habitat: Waste areas, fields and roadsides.

Blooms: June through October.

Range: Throughout North America.

Remarks: Also called Blue Sailors, it comes in blue, white and pink. A native of Europe and Asia, chicory has become a common though beautiful weed. The root can be roasted and ground as a coffee substitute.

My Observations

Date seen: _____

Locality: _____

Notes:

Asiatic Dayflower
Commelina communis

Sticker #28

Height: Creeper, stem 1 to 3 feet long.

Size of Flower: ½ to 1 inch.

Habitat: Roadsides, moist woodland soils, ditches and around homes.

Blooms: June to October.

Range: Wisconsin, Michigan, New York, southward to Alabama, west to Kansas.

Remarks: Flowers only bloom for one day, hence its name. An Asian import, it is regarded as a weed, but has been used as a salad herb.

My Observations

Date seen: _____

Locality: _____

Notes:

Larger Blue Flag
Iris versicolor

Sticker #29

Height: 2 to 3 feet.

Size of Flower: 3 inches.

Habitat: Wetlands, marshes, along pond and stream edges.

Blooms: May through August.

Range: Manitoba to southern Labrador, Minnesota, Wisconsin, Ohio, western Pennsylvania and Virginia.

Remarks: Iris species come in many beautiful colors, hence the name "Iris," from the Greek for rainbow. The rhizome (root) is poisonous, but has been used to cure bruises when ground into a powder and applied to wounds.

My Observations

Date seen: _____

Locality: _____

Notes:

Wild Lupine
Lupinus perennis

Sticker #30

Height: 8 inches to 2 feet.

Size of Flower: 1 inch.

Habitat: Clearings, dry sandy soil, meadows.

Blooms: Late spring to July.

Range: Ontario, Maine to Minnesota, Ohio, south to Florida, west to Louisiana and Missouri.

Remarks: Only lupine native to eastern United States and Canada. Fifty species in the west. This plant is a legume and enriches the soil it grows in. Also called Perennial Lupine.

My Observations

Date seen: _____

Locality: _____

Notes:

Forget-me-not
Myosotis scorpioides

Sticker #31

Height: 6 to 24 inches.

Size of Flower: ¼ to ⅓ inch.

Habitat: Borders of streams, ponds, brooksides and wet areas.

Blooms: May through October.

Range: Almost throughout.

Remarks: Presumably a European import, it is a favorite flower of lovers. Also called Mouse Ear and Scorpion Grass. Its tightly coiled buds resemble the tail of a scorpion, hence its Latin name.

My Observations

Date seen: _____

Locality: _____

Notes:

Virginia Bluebells
Mertensia virginica

Sticker #32

Height: 8 inches to 2 feet.

Size of Flower: ¾ to 1 inch.

Habitat: Rich, damp woodlands, bottomlands.

Blooms: March through early June.

Range: Minnesota, southern Ontario, New York, south to North Carolina, Alabama and west to eastern Kansas.

Remarks: Also called: Virginia Cowslip, Tree Lungwort and Oysterleaf. Spectacular show in woodlands in spring as it carpets the ground with pale blue flowers, although by summer there is no sign of either leaves or flowers.

My Observations

Date seen: _____

Locality: _____

Notes:

INDEX OF COMMON NAMES
References are to sticker numbers, not *page numbers.*

Asiatic Dayflower 28	Japanese Honeysuckle 6
Bird's-foot Violet 26	Larger Blue Flag 29
Black-eyed Susan 10	Northern Pitcher Plant 15
Bull Thistle 19	Oxeye Daisy 3
Butter-and-eggs 12	Pink Lady's Slipper 20
Cardinal Flower 17	Prickly Pear Cactus 8
Chicory 27	Purple Loosestrife 23
Common Buttercup 9	Queen Anne's Lace 5
Common Dandelion 7	Red Clover 22
Common Milkweed 24	Rugosa Rose 25
Common Sunflower 11	Shooting Star 21
Forget-me-not 31	Sweet Goldenrod 13
Fragrant Water Lily 2	Tiger Lily 14
Indian Paintbrush 18	Virginia Bluebells 32
Indian Pipe 4	Wild Columbine 16
Jack-in-the-Pulpit 1	Wild Lupine 30

INDEX OF SCIENTIFIC NAMES

References are to sticker numbers, not page numbers.

Aquilegia canadensis 16	*Lonicera japonica* 6
Arisaema triphyllum 1	*Lupinus perennis* 30
Asclepias syriaca 24	*Lythrum salicaria* 23
Castilleja coccinea 18	*Mertensia virginica* 32
Chrysanthemum leucanthemum .. 3	*Monotropa uniflora* 4
Cichorium intybus 27	*Myosotis scorpioides* 31
Cirsium vulgare 19	*Nymphaea odorata* 2
Commelina communis 28	*Opuntia humifusa* 8
Cypripedium acaule 20	*Ranunculus acris* 9
Daucus carota 5	*Rosa rugosa* 25
Dodecatheon meadia 21	*Rudbeckia hirta* 10
Helianthus annuus 11	*Sarracenia purpurea* 15
Iris versicolor 29	*Solidago odora* 13
Lilium tigrinum 14	*Taraxacum officinale* 7
Linaria vulgaris 12	*Trifolium pratense* 22
Lobelia cardinalis 17	*Viola pedata* 26